MAGIC TREE HOUSE®

MUMMIES IN THE MORNING

MARY POPE OSBORNE'S

MAGIC TREE HOUSE®

MUMMIES IN THE MORNING

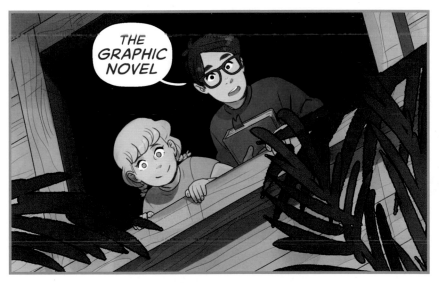

THE GRAPHIC NOVEL

ADAPTED BY

JENNY LAIRD

WITH ART BY

KELLY & NICHOLE MATTHEWS

A STEPPING STONE BOOK™

RANDOM HOUSE 🏠 NEW YORK

Text copyright © 2022 by Mary Pope Osborne
Art copyright © 2022 by Kelly Matthews & Nichole Matthews
Text adapted by Jenny.Laird

All rights reserved. Published in the United States by Random House Children's Books, a division
of Penguin Random House LLC, New York. Adapted from *Mummies in the Morning,* published by
Random House Children's Books, a division of Penguin Random House LLC, New York, in 1993.

Random House and the colophon are registered trademarks and A Stepping Stone Book
and the colophon are trademarks of Penguin Random House LLC. RH Graphic with
the book design is a trademark of Penguin Random House LLC. Magic Tree House
is a registered trademark of Mary Pope Osborne; used under license.

Visit us on the Web!
rhcbooks.com
MagicTreeHouse.com

Educators and librarians, for a variety of teaching tools, visit us at RHTeachersLibrarians.com

Library of Congress Cataloging-in-Publication Data is available upon request.
ISBN 978-0-593-17479-1 (pb) — ISBN 978-0-593-17476-0 (hc) —
ISBN 978-0-593-17477-7 (lib. bdg.) — ISBN 978-0-593-17478-4 (ebook)

The artists used Clip Studio Paint to create the illustrations for this book.
The text of this book is set in 13-point Cartoonist Hand Regular.

MANUFACTURED IN CHINA
10 9 8 7 6 5 4 3 2
First Graphic Novel Edition

This book has been officially leveled by using the F&P Text Level Gradient™ Leveling System.

To Georgia and Ada McCulloch
—M.P.O.

For Krish and Alya — a truly magical
brother-and-sister team
—J.L.

To April, our amazing art director, who
has been with us through thick and thin (and
deadlines). Thank you for everything you've
done to offer assistance and advice; this series
wouldn't be the same without you.
—K.M. & N.M.

CHAPTER ONE
Meow!

On a day like any other, in the woods not far from home, Jack and Annie found a mysterious tree house.

FROG CREEK

Hello?
Anybody
there?

The tree house started to spin.

It spun faster and faster.

CHAPTER TWO
Oh, Man. Mummies!

HUFF

PUFF

I think my glasses are getting sweaty.

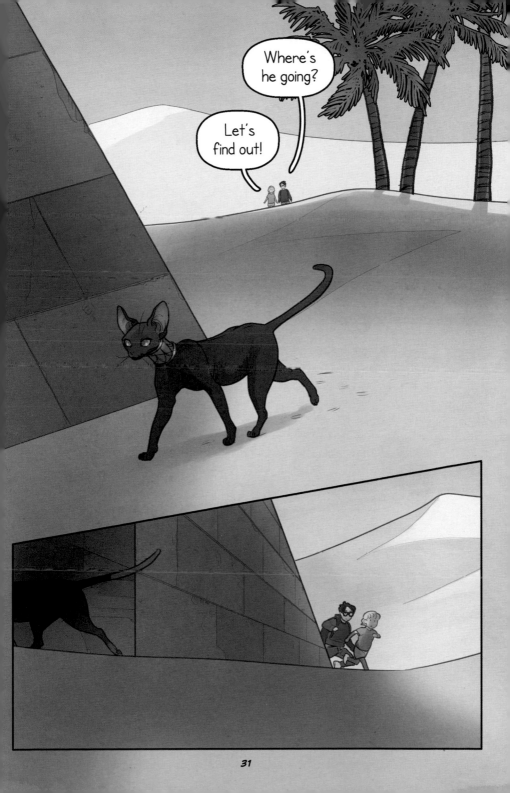

CHAPTER THREE
The Pyramid

The burial chamber is in the middle of the pyramid.

See?

It seems to be straight ahead.

CLATTER

CHAPTER FOUR
Back from the Dead

"Tomb robbers often stole the treasure buried with mummies.

False passages were sometimes built to stop the robbers."

No live mummy.

Just a tomb robber.

Yikes. A tomb robber?

CHAPTER FIVE
The Ghost-Queen

We saw a tomb robber earlier.

He was trying to steal your scepter but dropped it when he saw us.

If I do not find the book soon, I will never get to the Next Life.

Don't worry, we will help you find the book before the robber gets it.

Right, Jack?

Um. Right. But *how?*

My brother carved this secret message on the wall, telling me how to find it.

Where? Here?

Yes. He carved his message on the only stone in this wall shaped like the eye of a cat.

Cool.

What do these tiny pictures mean?

Alas, my brother forgot my strange problem. I cannot see clearly that which is close to my eyes.

I have not been able to read his message for a thousand years.

CHAPTER SIX
The Writing on the Wall

A folded cloth.

Well, not really.

But that is the hieroglyph for a folded cloth.

Hmmph.

I don't see how that's a folded cloth, but okay.

CHAPTER SEVEN
The Scroll

CREEAK

CHAPTER EIGHT
The Mummy

CHAPTER NINE
Follow the Leader

Where did we put the Pennsylvania book?

CHAPTER TEN
Another Clue

You're just in time for lunch.

Missed the first adventure? Get whisked back
to the time of dinosaurs with Jack and Annie in . . .

Where Is Here?

LET THE
MAGIC TREE HOUSE®
WHISK YOU AWAY!

Read all the novels in the #1 bestselling chapter book series of all time!

TRACK THE FACTS WITH JACK & ANNIE!

MARY POPE OSBORNE is the author of many novels, picture books, story collections, and nonfiction books. Her #1 *New York Times* bestselling Magic Tree House® series has been translated into numerous languages around the world. Highly recommended by parents and educators everywhere, the series introduces young readers to different cultures and times, as well as to the world's legacy of ancient myth and storytelling.

JENNY LAIRD is an award-winning playwright. She collaborates with Will Osborne and Randy Courts on creating musical theater adaptations of the Magic Tree House® series for both national and international audiences. Their work also includes shows for young performers, available through Music Theatre International's Broadway Junior® Collection. Currently the team is working on a Magic Tree House® animated television series.

KELLY & NICHOLE MATTHEWS are twin sisters and a comic-art team. They get to do their dream job every day, drawing comics for a living. They've worked with Boom Studios!, Archaia, the Jim Henson Company, Hiveworks, and now Random House!